Helgi
Explores the World

www.nbforlag.com

© Story: Njörður P. Njarðvík
© Illustrations: Halldór Pétursson
© Translation: John Porter

NB forlag
Printing: Oddi

1ˢᵗ Edition in English   2010
2ⁿᵈ Edition in English   2014

ISBN 978-9935-471-01-7

Helgi
Explores the World

Njörður P. Njarðvík & Halldór Pétursson

The world is a big place. It's bigger than the whole farm. It's so big that it takes near-ly a whole day to explore it all. There are so many things to see. There's the stream in the gully, the cliff where the birds are, the swan pool, the river, the mountain, the lava rocks and a whole lot more. Today Helgi is going to explore the whole world. His whole world, the one that he can see, the one that is all around him and that belongs to nobody but him. But he's not planning to go alone. His two best friends are going with him. They're not other children; they're a dog and a horse. The dog is called Merry, and the mare Fly. Helgi lives out in the country, you see. It's almost midsummer, and so it's just the right time to go and explore the world.

It's a bright, warm day. Helgi goes to his mother and tells her that he's setting out now to explore the world.

'Well now, Helgi', says his mother, 'then you'll have to remember to go carefully. The world's a big place, and there are many dangers hidden there. And you mustn't be too long, or we'll start to worry about you.'

'Don't worry about me, Mummy', says Helgi. 'It's my own world that I'm going to explore. Nothing can happen to me there. Merry and Fly are coming with me, too.'

So Helgi fetches Fly, leads her to the hen house, steps up on it and clambers on her back.

'Come on, Merry', Helgi calls to the dog. And so they set off.

They are all in a happy mood and rather proud of themselves, as you would expect, since they're going off to explore the world. Fly trots in a slow and dignified way down the path to the farm gate. Helgi smiles and waves goodbye with his cap like a seasoned traveller. And Merry patters along behind with his head up and tail cocked as he gazes admiringly at his master.

But not everyone is so delighted by this expedition. The hens run cackling out of the path as though they had been flung in all directions.

'What a fuss', says the rooster sulkily, as he escapes from under the horse's hooves. 'No good can come of such arrogance. They ought to go quietly and show more respect to others. A fellow can't even peck in peace on his own doorstep.'

And the pussycat sits on the hen house and narrows her yellow eyes at Merry. She's no friend of dogs, and thinks it disgraceful to see how Merry prances round that silly boy. 'Typical of dogs', she thinks. She is used to having her own adventures and does not let anyone tell her what to do.

To tell the truth, this expedition does not start at all well. In order to get down to the cliff where the birds are, you first have to cross the gully. And it's pretty deep. At least that's how it looks to Helgi. Fly is none too happy about scrambling down there, either. She stops abruptly when she comes to the edge. It happens so suddenly that Helgi is thrown forward off Fly's neck and tumbles head over heels into the gully. His cap and both his shoes fall off, and he lands on his backside down in the stream. He sits there howling, while Merry comes running up to look after his friend. He realises right away that comfort is called for here, so he licks Helgi's cheek reassuringly. Fly also clambers down into the gully and gives Helgi a friendly nuzzle on the ear, as if she's asking him to forgive her. But there's no consoling Helgi. Exploring the world is obviously hard work. He has hurt himself. Scratched his hands and bruised his back. And his bottom's wet too. He has half a mind to turn back. Go home to Mother and get some milk and cakes. He knows that can cure anything. But when he thinks a little more about it, he feels it would be rather shameful to give up and go home so soon. He's pretty sure that his big sister would laugh at him. Helgi doesn't like that idea at all.

So there's nothing else for it but to pull yourself together and carry on. Helgi wipes the tears from his eyes, staggers to his feet, and starts looking for his shoes. Merry finds one of them and brings it back triumphantly in his mouth. But Helgi is still so unhappy that he doesn't stroke him or praise him for being so clever. He leads Fly up out of the gully and clambers on her back. They go along slowly at first. Helgi is still feeling upset after his fall. And when Helgi is sad, Fly and Merry don't want to play.

But the weather is fine and there's a refreshing breeze from the sea. Before they know it, they are all back in a good mood. There's no point letting a little accident rob you of your courage. Fly quickens her pace and so they gallop along over the moor at breakneck speed towards the bird cliff. But all of a sudden the mare stops short, digs in all four hooves and jumps in the air, neighing with fright. Poor Helgi lurches forward on his nose onto the mare's neck and falls off on his backside again. Onto a large mound this time. Merry is so astonished that he sits down as dumb as a stone and stares petrified at this amazing sight.

All it took to frighten Fly so much was a little snipe that shot out from under the edge of the mound. He has his nest there by the mound and if he sees human beings, horses or dogs he flies away in fear of his life, beating his wings and chirping in alarm.

'I'm really surprised at you', Helgi says to Fly as soon as he gets to his feet again. 'Are you afraid of little birds?'

He gives the mare a friendly stroke and talks to her reassuringly. Now it's his turn to comfort his friend. Then he shows Merry the snipe's nest, but tells him not to go too near it. He's half ashamed of himself for having come across the moor at such speed, because there are lots of moorland birds living there.

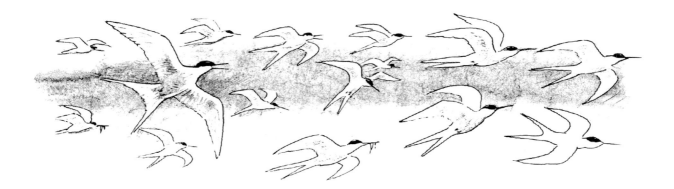

But the moorland birds are not the only creatures living in this place. Helgi has barely got started again when a huge flock of terns hurl themselves down at him, screeching furiously.

'Away with you, boy', screech the terns. 'Away with you all. We don't want you crashing about our nesting sites like this. We'll peck your heads if you don't beat it right away.'

One of the terns swoops down at Merry with a fearful scream, so he scurries under Fly's tummy, growling as he glares up in the air. But Helgi waves his cap over his head to defend himself against the terns' attack.

'What a noise', he mutters. 'You'd think these terns imagine they own the whole world.'

Then he clucks at Fly to go on, and they escape from the terns as quickly as they can.

Now they have reached the edge of the cliff. There's a fairly broad ledge leading down the cliff, and Helgi urges Fly forward. She's not too pleased about this. It's not just that she's afraid of heights, but also that the birds are making an unearthly racket. There are endless rows of seabirds sitting on jutting rocks and ledges, screeching and squawking at each other without a break, and flying all over the place. Helgi gets quite confused by all this noise and bustle.

'What impudence!' shrieks a razorbill, right under Fly's feet. 'No room for you here. Who gave you permission to come here and frighten birds from their nests? Do you think we like to have you here? What would you say if all us birds came home to your house?'

These were too many questions to be answered all at once. Helgi saw his best move would be to scramble back up to the edge of the cliff. He thought it was quite amusing to have been in among the crowd of birds, but he's relieved to be away from all the noise and hubbub. And he can scarcely imagine that it had done the birds much harm just because he had dropped in on his way round the world.

Not far above the cliff the screeching of the birds fades away, and soon it is so quiet that all you can hear is the whistling of the breeze in the meadow grass. They head up to the swan pool and all take a drink at the water's edge, where the farm stream flows out of the little lake.

On the lake there is a pair of swans that come there every spring to lay their eggs. They have just had their young now, and are teaching them to swim. As soon as the cob sets eyes on Helgi and Fly and Merry, he gets angry. He always imagines that everyone wants to attack his young ones. He comes raging up towards the bank and beats his wings against the water. The mother swan and the young ones follow behind him. Helgi sees that it would be best to run away, but it's not easy for him to mount the horse, because there are no mounds nearby. And just as Helgi manages to crawl onto Fly, the cob flies up on the mare's back and bites Helgi on the arm.

'I'll teach you not to attack my young ones', he hisses.

Helgi is trembling like a leaf. He doesn't understand these vicious threats. He didn't mean any harm. But he knows that this is not the place for him.

As soon as Helgi and Fly and Merry have escaped from the swans' clutches, they go on slowly for a while. It's midday now, and the weather has warmed up. Helgi takes off his scarf and ties it round Fly's neck, and holds his cap in his hand. He starts thinking about everything that has happened to him on the way here. It's as though he's always been getting in someone's way. Everywhere is full of life. And he can easily understand that the birds want to protect their eggs and their young. What would his mother say if someone tried to take him away from her? So he decides to be careful and make sure he doesn't frighten the animals that live in the world.

All at once the rain comes pelting down. The water streams down from the sky like a waterfall. And there's no shelter from the rain. But Helgi finds an answer to that. He jumps off the mare and crouches down under Fly's belly. Merry joins him there right away.

'Well now, Fly', Helgi says. 'What a wonderful creature you are, old girl. We can even use you as a house when it rains.'

Fly bends her big head down to Helgi and gives a quiet and friendly neigh, and allows him to stroke her cheek. Merry snuggles up alongside him. All three of them are such good friends.

As soon as the rain stops they set off again. Now the way lies up into the mountain. But first they have to cross the river. Helgi looks for a convenient spot, and soon finds a suitable ford. Fly wades slowly and carefully into the river. She knows that she'll have to watch her step. It's no less dangerous here than it was on the bird cliff. She doesn't want to drop Helgi off her back into the river.

All at once a shoal of salmon comes swimming up very fast. The salmon are running up the riverbed one behind the other and leaping the falls. They're hurrying up to the mountain lake in order to spawn. One salmon takes a huge leap and comes sailing over Helgi and Fly.

They can hear the sound his flight makes – 'Sssssssssss. Off, off, off. I'm in a hurry, hurry, hurry. Away, away, away.'

Then he disappears into the stream above the falls. Helgi sees the tail thrashing as the salmon vanishes into the wall of water above him. What a quick way to travel!

On the mountainside above the river there are huge boulders and great piles of rock scattered about. Helgi's grandma told him that in the old days a giantess used to live on the mountain, and one time she threw all these boulders down the slope in a fit of rage. Fortunately, the giantess died long ago, so Helgi is not afraid to be there. But he is very startled when he comes round one of the boulders and an enormous grey-brown head appears. It's not a giant's head, to be sure, but it's terrifying enough all the same, with staring eyes, and huge antlers with many branches. Fly falls down in a state of shock. She sinks on her haunches, and Helgi has to cling on

tight to her neck. A horse with horns? Not possible. It's a reindeer that's crossed their path so unexpectedly. A big bull reindeer with magnificent horns, ready to charge at anyone who disturbs his peace. But at the moment he's just as surprised as Fly is. The horse and the reindeer stare each other in the eye for a moment, then they both flee. Helgi is glad he's able to hang on.

The peak of the mountain sticks up in the sky like a great horn. Sometimes it's called Farmhorn. It's certainly a must to go there if you're exploring the world, because there's no better view than from up there. You can see far out to sea where the ships are sailing. And from there Helgi's farm looks no bigger than a mound. You feel big and powerful up on a high mountain, and everything else looks small. But the way up there is steep, and there's still some snow lying, even though it's summertime. There are no screeching terns, vicious swans or leaping salmon, only a few harmless sheep to be seen. Even so, it's no place for a little country boy. Not even if he's going to explore the whole world. The snow is wet and still a bit loose, and down below there's a precipice and a steep abyss. Suddenly the mare starts to slide on the snow. She goes slowly at first, but she speeds up fast and heads straight towards the edge of the crags. She digs her hooves in. Helgi pulls on the reins with all his might. Not only that, but Merry hangs onto Fly's tail with his teeth and tries with all his strength to stop the slide. Now for the first time on this adventure Merry is really afraid for his master. It was pretty easy getting past the birds and animals. But if Helgi tumbles over the crags, then he'll never come back to stroke and fondle him. Merry knows this because he's a clever dog. He pulls and pulls on Fly's tail. Finally she stops, right on the edge of the crag. They stand rooted to the spot at first, because they know they're still in danger of their lives. Then they try to inch their way very carefully up the snowy slope to a safe place. At last they dare to rest. Helgi is still shaking with fright. The mountain peak will have to wait for a better time.

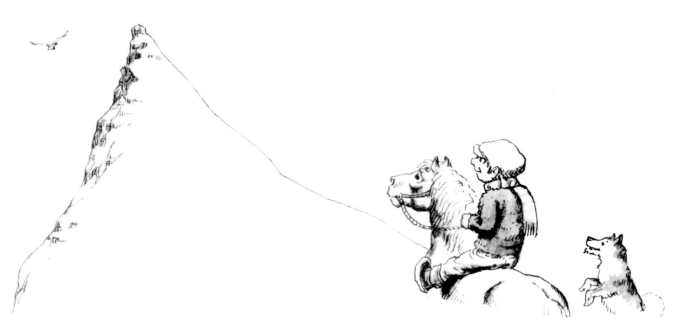

Now it's time to turn back and head for home. The borders of Helgi's world are the sea on one side and the mountain on the other. They have travelled almost from one end of the world to the other. The mountain peak still remains unconquered, but it doesn't matter. In fact it's good to have something left to explore later. They go out in front of the wall of crags and down the slope. Ahead they can see the path that leads back to the farm. There shouldn't be any danger from now on. They have got over their fright and are in the best of spirits again. But it's certainly not a good idea to boast of victory too soon. Up near the peak a tiny shadow can be seen in the sky. This shadow glides down through the sky with incredible speed, growing quickly bigger the nearer it gets. Helgi knows nothing about it until something seizes his scarf as though it were trying to lift him up into the air. There's a huge eagle hanging over him, with flapping wings and gaping beak, glaring at him.

'So you were going up to the peak to steal my babies!' hisses the eagle. 'It would serve you right if I took you with me and let my babies eat you.'

This is too much for Merry. He has just saved his best friend from mortal danger. In a flash he forgets all his fear and becomes furious. He jumps up in the air as if he's going to attack the eagle, and barks his fiercest bark. The eagle is so startled that he lets go his grip on the scarf and disappears as quickly as he came.

'He got just what he deserved', thinks Merry smugly, and trots proudly after Fly, who has started to gallop off along the path for home.

26

There's only one thing left now which cannot be missed, and that is to stop at the edge of the lava rocks just outside the farm. The lava is ancient and rough, and has had stuff growing on it for a long time. There are green mosses and patches of grass all over the place. Helgi has often played there, and has had fun looking at all the different kinds of shapes in the ever-changing forms of the lava. But now it's getting dark. The evening shadows stretch their long dark arms in over the edge of the lava, and then all at once it looks as though the lava turns into living shapes. It seems to Helgi that all around him there are giants waking up after their long day's sleep. He feels that they are crowding round him and even reaching out their paws for him. Perhaps it's only the sound of the wind, but he thinks one of the giants is saying:

'Now it's time for a little boy to go home. The world is a big place and it doesn't all belong to you, even if you think it does. When men are asleep, the night belongs to us. And it's better then if you stay out of our way.'

Finally, Helgi has come all the way back home. When he has closed the gate and crawled up on Fly's back again, he is so tired that he lies face down on the horse and falls asleep. He is richer for his experience. He knows now that the world does not belong to him alone. The world is full of life. The world belongs to the birds and the animals just as much as it does to him, and you have to show them respect and friendship. Everything that lives shares the world with him, with the same rights as him. Helgi can sleep peacefully now, because he has come back to his own place. And that is good.

Merry scratches at the door and barks politely for someone to open up for them.

The cat looks down from the roof.

'It's that stupid dog come back', she thinks. 'No more peace now.'

The rooster struts outside the door with his hens.

'Well', he crows. 'So they're back home. Not so cocky now as when they rushed down the path this morning in all their pride. Maybe a fellow will be able to peck up his food in peace now.'

And in the window there's a hint of a smile on big sister's face.

Helgi is born

In early 1976, Jón Karlsson from the publisher Iðunn showed me some drawings by Halldór Pétursson. They were all of a boy, a horse and a dog in different situations in Icelandic nature. Jón asked me if I could write a story based on the pictures.

So I went to Halldór and asked him whether he had an idea for a story in mind. He said that he didn't, that he just wanted to draw a regular Icelandic farm boy.

I began shuffling the drawings like cards and chatted about them with my daughters, then five and six years old. When we came to the picture of the Arctic terns diving over the boy and his friends, one of the girls defended the birds' actions by pointing out that the boy was trespassing on their land.

Then the idea came to me that everywhere these friends went, they were running into creatures that wanted to be left in peace.

This sparked the next idea about a journey through the boy's world. Thus we found our story. The theme was respect for all life and for nature itself. When the story was ready, Halldór added a few more pictures and a map of Helgi's world. Now Helgi was on his feet and off to explore the world.

Njörður P. Njarðvík